LORETTA TRONI

AND THE BLUE SKY BEYOND

Thirty-Three Little Fables

Illustrations by Anna Savio

MERLINO

Revised English edition first published 2010
by Merlino
125 St. Ann's Close
Newcastle upon Tyne, England
Tel: 07770 518 149
E-mail: tronilorretta@hotmail.com

First published in Italian in 1988
by La Serinissima, Italy

Front cover and illustrations: Anna Savio for Loretta Troni.
English translation: Malcolm King
Revision and corrections: John Jones
Typesetting and printing by Flying Colours, Beamish, Co. Durham, England.

ISBN 978-0-9564947-0-2

To my beloved children, Marco and Stefania

Even as a child I learned to play a mental game with the experiences – often cruel experiences – of my life, interpreting them in my own special way.

"I'm living through these moments," I would say to myself, "but I know that life is not only like this. Beyond it all there is the blue of the sky, there are flowers in the fields, children laughing, adults capable of loving," even if these were experiences I had not had.

Over the years, I have lived through, and seen, disease and other situations which can silence the voice of the heart but my desire for beauty and tranquillity only has grown with time.

It was enjoyable to write these little stories, where even the most ordinary happenings in the lives of the nice, wise people around me can be transformed into something else.

I would like to take the opportunity to thank Dina Visona who encouraged me to go on writing; Antonio Brazzale dei Paoli for his useful suggestions during the preparation of these stories; Anna Savio for illustrating this book so sensitively; and my friend, Luisa Farina, who has accompanied me throughout this experience.

FATHER CHRISTMAS'S PRESENT
THE STAR AND THE YOUNG HORSE
CHIARA
THE ENCHANTED CASTLE
HOW SILENCE GAVE ME MY VOICE
CARLO THE ACROBAT
TALKING TO THE SEA
MOTHER LUCIA'S GIFT

FATHER CHRISTMAS'S PRESENT

One year, late on Christmas Eve, Father Christmas stopped at a remote country village where there was an orphanage. Every child received a special gift. In the middle of the main room the children discovered a great basket which gave out light. Inside, there were thousands of little coloured parcels tied with big ribbons, each with a child's name on.

Everyone had more than one present. Around the basket was a coloured band on which was written:

"No one can ever take away what is yours and yours alone."

They all searched for their presents and with their little arms happily held them close to their heart or up to their cheeks to feel the warmth of them.

With trembling hands I opened mine...One, two three: they were *art, love* and *the will to live.*

I assure you that they are all still with me.

THE STAR AND THE YOUNG HORSE

I was sitting on the beach one day gazing at the sea when I suddenly spotted – right in front of me and not very far away – a sea-horse and a starfish. I started studying them but almost immediately looked away because I realised they were talking and I felt like an intruder.

I turned to look at the sea again, amazed at what I had witnessed.

I've often been astonished at the different languages that nature speaks to the attentive ear but this was the first time I'd heard a starfish and a sea-horse talking. In silence I went on looking straight ahead and after a while I felt my hand being stroked.

After a moment they asked me if I would like to hear a story they wanted to tell me. I was only too happy to accept.

The little sea-horse explained that a long while ago he had been a real horse, beautiful but lonely. Every evening as he looked at the sky before going to sleep, it seemed to him that up there a star was gazing intensely at him. To her he recounted his dreams, his sadness and his joy.

From all that distance away the star replied, shining even more brightly and revealing to him how much she wanted to come down to the Earth to get to know that marvellous place that she could only see from afar.

She explained to him that beyond the beautiful Green Valley where he lived, there were mountains, seas, other valleys, glaciers, deserts…a whole world he didn't know about and which she alone could see from above.

They talked together of their feelings and emotions and in this exchange they completed each other: the one saw what the other touched.

They both wished they could be together much more but they knew that in order to achieve that they would both have to take a very important step: they would have to run the risk of changing and of facing an unknown world.

How could a star, which was in fact an immense sun, come close to the Earth?

How could a horse jump into space?

At last they decided on a place where both of them would be united, if only they were capable of changing – an unfamiliar place where they would be able to live their new life together.

The great love that they had for each other rewarded them by giving them the power to transform themselves.

And so they found themselves there on the beach, she now a Starfish and he a Sea-horse. So close that they could finally touch each other and not have to wait for night to see each other. Day and night eternity was with them.

They looked at the sea, unknown and immense which was to be their world forever.

As I stroked them affectionately, I told them how much I admired them and wished them great happiness.

On the beach, kissed by the sun, they were shining with the colour of joy and together they disappeared into the sea.

CHIARA

While she was still a little girl, Chiara was stung by an insect.

Her arm swelled up and after a few hours she fell into a deep sleep.

Her parents were alarmed and called the doctor who, after examining her, suggested she should go to hospital for further check-ups.

Chiara slept almost the whole time, she awoke only for short periods, just long enough to eat but never even managed to take off her pyjamas before falling asleep again.

They did various tests and all of them turned out negative. The doctors didn't know how to explain Chiara's reaction to the sting. "It seems almost as if she'd been stung not in her arm but in her soul, in her innermost feelings," said the chief physician of the hospital.

After other vain attempts to find a diagnosis they advised the parents to take her home.

From time to time she was examined by different doctors who always found her physically healthy.

Her mother took her into the garden when she was awake and sat her in a deck-chair.

"Chiara, just look: there's the swing waiting for you; there are your friends to play with; there are so many beautiful things all around you," she encouraged her daughter but she only got this reply:

"Yes, it's lovely, I'd really like to but I can't, I'm sleepy, I can't cope" and she plunged into sleep again.

When her birthday arrived, she was given a tiny little kitten. Chiara looked at it happily but after a bit she said: "Lovely, thank you but you play with it yourselves, I'm sleepy."

"Oh no!" said her mother, "It was given to you and you have to look after it, otherwise leave it to die, if that's how you feel."

They put the kitten on her lap and went off into the house. The kitten didn't stir and you couldn't hear its miaow because it was so small. It licked and licked at Chiara's hands and clothes. She realised that the poor thing was hungry and that she had to do something for it. With great difficulty she managed to start keeping her eyes open – everything in her was stiff and asleep – but looking at the kitten she forgot to think about it. She got up to fetch it a bit of milk. She walked cautiously, slowly, the kitten was in no hurry.

She became very attached to it and gradually came back to being a lively and vivacious girl.

I met Chiara a little while ago and after having told me her story she asked me: "Weren't you ever stung by an insect?"

THE ENCHANTED CASTLE

Ever since I was born I've lived in a most beautiful castle: its walls with their deep foundations are thick and robust. It has spacious rooms and many towers.

A special thing about it: it's magic and so I call it the "Enchanted Castle."

You should know that from one of its big towers you can see the sun rising behind the mountains and from the other side you can watch the sunset over the sea.

On the other hand, some days you can see the sun rise above the sea and the sunset behind the mountains.

From the north tower you can see winter, from the south summer, from the west autumn and from the east spring.

When you go up on the castle battlements at night you see a sky that has no equal: a dome of stars wraps you in deepest blue, lit by the moon.

I sleep in a comfortable bedroom which has a huge piece of furniture with many drawers and if you go close you can read the word "Dreams" written on it.

In the kitchen, warm and welcoming, you find all the bounty of the world, an ever-burning fire which heats the heart of the castle. There are many other rooms but all of them without doors. There is a single great door at the entrance which at one time was always kept locked.

Ever since I was little I would wander around happily, familiar with most of the castle. However there were so many rooms, I still have'nt got to know all of them.

For a long time I was drawn to the more colourful and noisy ones: I got to know certain rooms very well, for instance the room marked "Fear", a place full of lightning and thunder, monsters and all the things that terrify you;

the music room with the word "Harmony" on the door, with melodious sounds coming from it, which have always given me a sense of peace;

the room of the "Unexpected", where I knew that the most unimaginable things were projected on a screen;

the room of "Anger" from which issued a constant black smoke;

the room of the "Sounds", from which you heard endless noises, laughter and chatting…

Rooms of every kind, with huge windows through which unfamiliar things were always entering, accompanied by strange smells, noises and the voices of people wandering around outside, who were staying in the neighbourhood and commenting on the castle.

So I decided to put in doors but I only blocked up the rooms and you couldn't breathe.

I took off the doors but then all the clutter in the rooms spilled out into the corridors.

The years passed and the confusion got worse, until one day I understood: I even took off the great main door and finally the surplus from all the rooms flew out, never to return.

From that day on I have wanted neither keys nor doors.

HOW SILENCE GAVE ME MY VOICE

When I was born, even my very first cries were regarded as a kind of language. Later, my sing-songs were moulded into words with which to name everything.

As I grew up they taught me how to use sentences properly in order to be understood.

I was taught what one is allowed to say and what one must not even think.

Schools, parents, all the situations of life, have always demanded a so-called comprehensible, correct use of language for communication.

As the years went by I had the feeling that even though I was very good at using words, I never said anything of my own.

"What would the natural tones of my voice be like?" I asked myself for a long while. I realised that even in talking to myself I used the same forms as I used with other people.

I went far and wide in life searching for professors, enlightened people. I read books of all sorts from Micky Mouse to Freud: so many, many words, in every language, in every conceivable way but none of them lead me anywhere.

So I sought out places where the human voice was not to be heard: in the woods, among the plants, on the plains, on the beach, by the sea, in the sky…At last, falling deep into silence, I could feel myself. They and I, in harmony – with the simple primordial sounds of nature, her utterances, her silences. There my voice found its own worth, found its form and from the great teachings of nature I slowly learned to find the right cadences and to express myself with simplicity.

The wind doesn't ask permission to speak, it is both strong and soft. The rain's chatter is sometimes vigorous, sometimes delicate as it touches the earth, perhaps telling the tree where it has come from.

The sun speaks with its warmth.

There is room for every element in Nature, each with its own voice.

I, a human being, am learning from these great sages how to really express myself.

CARLO THE ACROBAT

I haven't seen Carlo for a long time, it always gives me a
warm feeling to think about him and remember such a sym-
pathetic friend.

He loved to travel around from one country to another
and the type of work he did made this possible.

One thing that struck me when I met him, were his big
sweet boyish eyes, clear pools in his strong athletic body.
His elegant agility was surprising but he hadn't always
been like this.

At one time he had been travelling, moving around from
region to region he explained but his mind stayed attached
to a particular way of life that he had enjoyed for only a
short time.

He recounted how in his very first years he had lived in a
comfortable country house and how he could still remember its sounds and smells.

As the child of an acrobat father and skater mother, he had
lived the life of the circus from the very beginning. The
house was always a bustle of different people, each one
with his own speciality in the family circus. From being a
small child he was trained as a little athlete and he rapidly
began to fly from one trapeze to another with great skill.

So he started to travel from place to place, seeing less and
less of the big old house.

For a few years this moving around fascinated him and he

was much intrigued by the novelty and variety of the countries and cities he saw. After a while however he realised
that, forced as he was always to move on, it was a problem
if he became attached to the places he stayed in and it was
difficult to make friends of any kind. Nothing was stable or
lasted more than a few days. He had the feeling of only just
touching the surface of things, places, or people, without
experiencing them to the full.

Bit by bit he began to feel nostalgic for the house where he
was born. The only place where, when he opened the window in the morning, he could see in front of him the same
plants as the day before and watch them grow and change
with the seasons.

He was very sad and heard the audience's applause as a
hollow metallic noise which gave him no warmth.

He saw so many faces, so many smiles but for whom? For
him or for the acrobat? He felt anonymous.

His body exhibited the physical elasticity of many years'
training but inside himself he felt so confused he no longer
even knew if he liked being an acrobat.

He needed to be alone with himself and reflect.

He thought it only right that he should talk about his state
of mind to his parents, who being proud of his virtuosity
had taken it for granted that their son should follow the
family tradition.

Although disappointed, they understood and let Carlo go
back to the place of his childhood.

When he got there, even before he went inside his eyes
had embraced with joy the house and the valley where he
was born.

At first he was overcome with excitement after that gave
way to days of immense serenity and peace.

It was all so familiar and so beautiful! as he started to relax he felt all the old emotions and feelings coming back to him: they hadn't vanished! They were there inside him.

He loved that place even more for the part of him that he had left there. But after a while, when he thought about it, he began to understand: he really did love his work, it was the kind of life he was forced to lead that disturbed him.

He started faithfully revisiting all the places in his village and its surroundings. By now he recognised every corner, every path of the countryside and the people recognised him. Sometimes he would stop and talk to the farm-workers and they remembered him as a child, a playfriend of their children.

He realised then that living for many years far away from his village had not cancelled out his memory from those people's minds. They recalled how he had been as a young boy and observed him now as an adult with curiosity.

Coming back home for the hundredth time after seeing an old friend, he realised that his memories of all the places he had been to and lived in, were just as important as the place of his childhood roots. Practically everywhere, come to think of it, there was somebody who could remember him.

It wasn't important to stay in one spot, it was how you lived while you were there; how you lived with yourself and with others. All those different places were the mosaic of his life and he could go back to them and always find someone with whom he had been friends.

Moving around was fine but better still was the spirit in which you did it. In each place he could find new faces and talk about his life; friends to listen to and to remember.

He had a great love for his work. When I got to know him he was happy to have met me and I know that one day or another I will meet him again.

I could even go and find him myself.

TALKING TO THE SEA

"Hello, Sea! I've been watching from the beach for twelve days but only now, walking right at the water's edge, can I hear your voice. Here your sounds manage to cover the noise the people make. Your movements are so strong and deafening! Perhaps that's why I noticed you today..."

"Are you male or female?"

"Is it important for you to know?"

"No, I suppose not."

I watch its continuous motion: strong, generous, open, deep. It's wonderful standing there and looking!

Changing the direction of my gaze, I see the sky and the hills behind me with that same intensity and boundlessness and my breathing becomes freer, deeper. It's good to have one's feet firmly planted in the sand and see these wonders all around and at the same time be part of them.

My eyes turn again towards the sea and at once I noticed my shadow lengthening over the water. As I watch, I see myself in a mirror but I see something else there, I see the outlines of my soul.

My body and my mind melt; I see my shadow changing, expanding and the waves that touch it now from the left, now from the right, a feeling of restfulness comes over me.

"I'm surprised, Sea, to find that there are no barriers between us and that your movements don't cancel out my shadow."

"Why? Should they?"

"You're so strong, big and vast, but yet so delicate."

Silence...I walk up and down for a bit.

" How good this is, so enjoyable!...

You know, sometimes I'm afraid of you because I think if I go in too deep I could drown. I would really like to let myself go, abandon myself to you, let myself be stroked by your soft motion."

"You can have whatever experience you want with me."

"You're so unemotional!..."

The sea laughs mockingly. At first I laugh too but then become serious again.

"But don't you ever stop, don't you ever rest, don't you ever sleep?"

"I'm sleeping, moving, playing and doing many other things all at the same time. I'm not part of Time as you understand it."

"Of course, you're eternal."

"Not exactly. I was born when the Earth was formed and will die with it."

"But you live so long, whereas we humans…"

"You live in the dimension of time."

"I don't understand."

Silence…It's true, I realise, that there are many ways of being on this earth.

"Your water is a body which doesn't grow old however."

"Nor does what you call your soul. Maybe thought exists more in Time."

"And where is your thought?"

"In the time I live through my movement."

"But why is our thought not matched to our body? Our body grows old, while our thought would want to do many things which …"

I interrupt myself.

"Hey!" I shout, "I didn't choose to live in this body, any

more than you chose to be the sea."

Silence.

"But you have to admit, your life on this earth is long."

"Your Time has nothing to do with me."

"Oh yes, I forgot."

After a while I try again.

"At night you scare me, you're so black."

"Tell me, then, do you also get scared of other colours?"

"So you're laughing at me?"

"I would never take the liberty of doing that."

I stop to think.

"You know so much!"

"No more than you. I just know how to observe."

"Have you ever wanted to be something else?"

"But really, you want to know everything! Now I'm the sea."

I observe the sea for a long time, wanting to feel inside me what it is saying to me and I get the impression that a great smile skims over the surface of the waves.

"Are you smiling at me?"

"I really like you," it replies.

"Me too."

I stay for a long time in silence, watching the sea, then I move away. After a while I retrace my steps.

"I have to say goodbye, I'm leaving tomorrow."

"So I'll say goodbye too."

I think to myself:

"Who knows if he cares at all; if what I seem to hear him say isn't just the fruit of my imagination."

I look at the sea impersonally and see only a mass of moving water, which will go on moving after I'm gone. But suddenly:

"Come back soon, I need you."

"*You* need *me*?" I ask.

"Yes", comes the reply, "I am the sea, I know many things but I also need people."

"And what about the fish?" I enquire.

"They are born and die inside me. You are out there."

"You mean you need to experience emotion and feelings, even though you're so different?"

He looks at me and I sense that it's no use using words, we communicate in a language which has no frontiers, no dimensions. Now it comes to me that everything, however diverse, is linked to everything else. The sea to the earth, people to the earth - everything is an exchange; and this can give joy, grief or indifference depending on how you live, if you live everything with your heart.

I immerse my feet in the water and let myself be washed, bathed, refreshed, pampered, stroked, charged by its power. I abandon myself to the sea in a fusion of pleasure…then after a while I move away.

"Goodbye, Sea!"

MOTHER LUCIA'S GIFT

There was once a mother – her name was Lucia – who had not given her daughter the normal necessities of life, because she was very poor and sick.

She had however given the child a lamp, which the little girl would turn on whenever she wanted to write.

Onto the bright page the girl would copy the phrases that she saw coming magically out of the lamp. The words of those phrases corresponded exactly to the most intimate feelings of her soul, that gave her a sense of warm and tender contact: it was as if her mother were close to her.

A few days ago, on a large sheet of paper, she wrote:

"The heart has no words..."

"The heart has..."

"Love has no words..."

"Love is an ever-burning lamp."

WHAT IF...
MARTA AND THE FABLES
THE SOLITARY PRINCESS
MASSIMO
GETTING TO KNOW AUTUMN
THE WONDERFUL CYCLE OF LIFE
THE GIANT WITH THE HUGE MOUTH

WHAT IF...

Pierluigi the elf was small, very small. A long time ago he had left his home, which was in a village on the edge of the woods.

He had been happy with his family until one day a flood from persistent rains had submerged his village. His parents, swept away by the water, were never found, neither they nor his other relatives. There were a few survivors, bewildered elves with wide eyes staring at the sky and asking themselves: "Why?"

Full of grief he had gathered his few things and set off.

Pierluigi couldn't bear to look, he couldn't stay to feel the pain inside himself and all around him. So he left, taking with him a ball as a souvenir of his childhood.

He lived as a ballad-singer, telling the story of a village that had existed far away over there, in a happy family – a village of happiness – for that was how he'd felt when he had lived there.

He was full of sadness and memories, even if every now and then he would try to make people smile, telling different stories and trying not to think of what was once for him, of lost happiness.

Nothing interested him any more, so wherever he went he never stayed longer than a week. Grief would overcome him and force him to leave.

In his wanderings he realised that he was searching for

somewhere as beautiful, as joyous as his lost village. If only someone would love him as they had then; he was afraid of becoming fond of anyone, of losing the people he loved.

So his life was full of conflict and he went on and on until one day he came to a village where the people were even more footloose than he, constantly travelling, constantly new faces.

But whatever could this place be with such movement?

He discovered the answer when he saw the sea open out before him – an immense stretch of water, something he'd never seen; so many people just passing through, while others stayed. There was a big port with ships arriving laden with hundreds of people, more than there had been in his entire village, more than he'd ever seen. He stopped astonished.

Here was something bigger than him and perhaps even bigger than his pain.

He chose a little house near the sea and for days watched everything around him with interest. There was such bustle and such a diversity of people, that after a bit he realised that he had no time to think of his regrets.

He no longer knew who he was. The pain he had carried around with him all those years had become his identity.

In this new world he felt bewildered and lost, suffocated by a sense of emptiness. The only thing he remembered about himself was the joy of his childhood and then so much pain. He took his ball and turned it over in his hands. He was still very scared.

Should he go back to those remote villages where his old identity was secure and intact? Or stay where he was and let himself live in this great world?

The days passed and the questions he asked himself were

many. His eyes would seek out his old ball less and less often, so one day he took it up and went out.

He went to a park where there were many children and played and played with them, like one of them. At a certain point rapid images, like scenes in a film, passed in front of his eyes. A thousand feelings went through him; he let them all come out of his mind, out of his body and he wept, at first tears of grief, of nostalgia. Then looking at those children and seeing their expressions as they watched the coloured ball turning and turning, he felt liberated.

Some of them came close to catch the ball but if they caught it badly it rolled away. One of them, however, grabbing it with both hands managed to grasp it and hold it tight. Holding the present moment entirely, like life!

The children's eyes shone happily when they held the ball firmly in their hands and then they just let it roll away to play another game.

"What if…this was the secret of life?" Pierluigi asked himself.

"What if I let go my past like a ball rolling away?"

"What if I took up a new game?"

"What if in my life I learnt to play many games, perhaps with other children, other people, other elves? I would be sharing those games with someone else and also my joys and my feelings.

He stayed in that big town where the sea was huge, a place in the world, which contains many elves, many people, many games and many "what ifs". And in particular, Pierluigi realised, it contained the adventure of his own life.

MARTA AND THE FABLES

Marta was a sweet and very lively child who adored reading fables.

She heard the adults say that fables are products of the imagination, they aren't real, they are only good for calming down children.

Marta thought otherwise.

In every fable she would recognise a child's dream, so she respected them and would read them most attentively, always finding new things that touched her.

All the fairies, magicians, gnomes, talking animals, weren't just fantasy for her. With the sensitivity of a child, she thought that fables were the most beautiful way to talk about people's most hidden desires, about their unrealised dreams. So she decided to live her own fable, making sure that dreams and imagination were always part of her life.

THE SOLITARY PRINCESS

I only heard about her when she was already grown-up. I was struck in particular by the fact that she carried with her something called "misfortune" or "fate". Convinced as I was that this was nothing but gossip, I decided to get to know the story of her life better, gathering the necessary information myself.

It's a well known fact that news-coverage in the papers, radio and TV alters and often gives distorted versions of people's lives.

When she was still a child both her parents died, leaving her an orphan. Her sister, older by at least fifteen years, had married and acceded to the throne to govern with her husband.

The little girl was educated and watched by governesses, for the most part strict and severe, who had no idea how to give her the attention, affection and the tenderness all children need.

Her childhood and adolescence had been pretty sad and so as not to add to the worries of her elder sister, who already had an important job to do as queen, she tried to be good, polite and kind. She applied herself to her studies without any fuss and was always smiling, but inside herself she was sad.

When she found herself alone she would dream and long for an embrace, a warm and affectionate hand to stroke her and someone to whom she could confide her hopes and desires, great or small.

Very soon she realised that crying didn't get her anywhere and her face began to get hard and sad-looking.

Affection was an absolute necessity for her and without it she felt a deep pain which she was powerless to do anything about.

Her sister told her that after all she is growing up and behaving like a child was useless and that she should learn to be independent not asking anything from anybody. So in time she shut herself up more and more.

When she was by herself, she would sing. She had studied singing and loved it. It was the only thing that pleased her and which she felt to be hers. So often, as she sang her sweet, sad songs, she would feel a little less unhappy.

Sometimes she would observe the people around her. They had made her life a thing of timetables and study; it was well organised and managed but it had no expression, no vitality.

She would feed on the poetry and music which nature offers: a rainbow, a bird's song, a butterfly in flight, the marvellous colours of the flowers; games she would play by herself; solitary explorations in the countryside.

She gazed in wonder at the flight of a kite guided only by the string which a child was holding in his hand: the little boy was smiling – admittedly poor, badly dressed and with no shoes - but with a smile and a sparkle in his eyes.

She felt such a longing for tenderness when she saw a mother giving her child a pat on the cheek, or drying his tears. Watching children of her own age and comparing them with how she lived, made her feel shut out from the world. In fact the children called her the "solitary princess."

So as not to show herself timid and sad and no longer able

to put up with the difference between herself and others, she started to hide herself away and fell into apathy. She didn't want to see for fear of suffering.

Of love she knew very little and if as a child she had lacked affection, as an adolescent it became even more a matter of necessity. Seeing her body changing she would have liked to have someone to tell her what it meant to become a woman and an adult. It seemed that only she felt everything to be so new and difficult, whereas for the others it was just natural.

Her strict education had ended by making her feel ashamed of herself; she grew up concealing her body and even her soul – with all those wonderful nuances of her being, like a flower that opens with the morning dew – kept hidden.

And as an adult she went on searching and waiting for the affection she had never received as a child, because she had no idea what it meant to love oneself. She kept on hoping her fate would change; that she would meet someone who would love her and in that way make her feel that she was worth something.

She was grown up by now so very soon it was decided at the palace to wed her to a prince of a neighbouring kingdom.

This arranged marriage certainly didn't help her. It gave her the sensation that everything followed an inevitable course, a fate she could not avoid.

She married the prince and got to the point of thinking she loved him for the small attentions she received – for that she was grateful.

Then she had a son, who brought her a whole world of wonderful sensations.

She was a mother with a heart of a child, who gave everything in herself to her son.

She taught her son that loving yourself means that you didn't have to feel lonely if your mother wasn't there; loving yourself means believing in your own abilities, knowing that you're doing what you can; asking yourself "Could I have done things differently? Did I really get it wrong?"

This she did instinctively with love and it filled much of the emptiness in her. By bringing him up like this, she was gradually teaching him to love himself. She asked herself if in doing so she was making a mistake but she didn't want her child to grow up in the solitude she had experienced. Gradually she realised that not having received love herself - that precious thing which had been denied her – it was important to learn to love oneself.

She began to understand that it was human to cry and make mistakes and so in educating her son she discovered she was educating herself; if she learned to give herself love there was no place for solitude.

What better teacher could there be than the past experiences of her own life, which she was now using wisely to live in the present?.

Her husband watched her change, become open and alive. Now she attracted the attention and interest of many people. She began to feel good choosing her own company and the friendship of people she found stimulating and comfortable to be with.

Very soon the nickname "solitary princess" disappeared.

Her marriage? I don't know whether it still is, or if it is ended. The story so far is beautiful enough, do you really want to know more?

MASSIMO

I want to tell you about Massimo, a child I got to know a while ago. He really loved life, he was always on the move, and he loved to play; but he only played with dangerous things, that was his problem!

For him if there wasn't a risk or danger it wasn't a good game. He often hurt himself and would run to his mother wailing. His mother would console him and advise him to play in other ways, for instance not playing the kind of games that he knew would result in cuts and bruises.

Ordinary games didn't inspire him even though they were no less fun – Massimo had to hurt himself in order to feel that it was a real game.

But as time passed there was no pleasure left in his games, because he only felt the pain he was giving himself.

He would have liked to get involved and try out other games and experience them, but not knowing how, he started to observe the other children and saw that each of them played in his own way. So he made his own choices, re-alising that even playing differently his own lively nature could express itself fully and freely. What was important was to have fun and take pleasure in what you were doing.

His mother, once so necessary as his figure of consolation, observed his decision with joy.

Massimo recognised that his mother could console him, share things with him, understand him but that he had to make his own mind up about how he chose to live.

GETTING TO KNOW AUTUMN

Normally you think you know the person you're used to having around, so you take things for granted and just go through the motions.

This is the kind of relationship one has with the things one sees every day. So one day I decided to stop and take a step backwards. I wanted to try to observe things more deeply, to look inside them.

To put my plan to the test I chose Nature, my inspiration and muse, advisor and friend.

It was the autumn season, fascinating, glowing with colour, showing itself in its splendid robes, giving out perfumes of wood, chestnuts and burning fires.

I was out walking in the park and after a bit decided to sit down on a sunny bench. I thought I was alone but all of a sudden voices around me claimed my attention.

From a huge, wonderfully coloured tree with heavy branches full of golden and yellow leaves, out darted an elf dressed in a thousand colours, who immediately made me think of Harlequin.

He danced around jumping in all directions, smiling and never once stopping.

I asked who he was and he replied that he was the Spirit of Autumn.

I watched him fascinated while he came closer and closer. He was wearing so many colours that no painter could ever have captured them on canvas.

"You're so lively!" I observed.

Smiling, he said: "I've just said goodbye to my friend Summer who's gone off to other countries."

"Isn't it a bit sad to be Autumn?" I asked. "Soon you'll have to lose all your colours and give way to Winter and you will be no more."

"Look around you," he said, and vanished.

"He's a bit mad," I thought.

For a bit I didn't think about anything. I looked and looked…Everything was so alive and colourful. I looked everywhere. Eventually my eyes came to rest on a small tree in front of me which was gradually becoming bare. I was struck by how a leaf would detach itself from its branch and fall so softly, spinning round, until it joined the others on the ground.

Looking closer, I could see leaves, fallen a while ago, that were becoming drier and drier and others already broken up and mixing with the earth.

At this point my friend "Harlequin" jumped out and asked me, laughing: "Did you see? So what do you think, do the leaves die?"

"No, I really don't think they do," I replied.

"You see" he told me, "I dance, jump and am happy because this is the time that nature lets all her flowers, fruits and leaves go and gives them to the earth, who like a mother, is waiting to hold them inside her."

"But don't they get dissolved under there?" I asked.

"What do you think earth would be like without all these other parts of nature in it?"

"It would be lacking some vital substances," I observed.

"Exactly. For example, the leaf's cycle goes on, it lets itself rest in the earth, become part of the Earth it came from."

"I see, so it doesn't die."

"Definitely not, it's just stopped being on that branch. Now in another form, drying out, mixing with the Earth, its existence continues."

"Things never cease to amaze me. Thank you, my elf friend."

"Don't ever forget the colours."

"What colours?"

"The colours of life," and he disappeared.

THE WONDERFUL CYCLE OF LIFE

I used to live holding tight to the people and experiences I didn't think I could do without.

I even held my breath so that pleasurable sensations or events or emotions shouldn't escape me.

And if I was suffering about something, I would despair that time wasn't taking it away fast enough. I would do anything rather than look inside myself and experience those moments.

I walked on tiptoe, just barely touching the surface of life and in this way the years passed and I would look at myself in the mirror less and less.

Supposing I wasn't as beautiful as I had been once?

I didn't like it if the sun was too hot or if it rained too much or if it was too hot or too cold or if it was foggy – everything was miserable.

But one day a kind man came to water this arid ground of mine.

The water was abundant and thirst-quenching and I drank deeply. I let all the parts that had by now been blocked soak up the water and then I started to stretch myself.

I asked who he was. He replied that he represented the four seasons.

I listened…He told me that *Spring* gives vent to all the sounds of life. *Summer* explodes into all its colours. *Autumn* happily says goodbye to the migrating birds and the leaves falling from the trees, which will give way to the seeds that in *Winter* will sleep under the snow protected by the cold.

"Drink at this fountain of wisdom;" he advised me, "and you will understand the cycle of your life."

THE GIANT WITH THE HUGE MOUTH

Years ago I knew a giant, not one out of my imagination or dreams, but a real one.

I had realised that life was something enormous, maybe too vast for me and I compared it to a giant.

How do you live with a giant? How can you cope with someone so immense?

I was too short to see him properly, if I went to the top of a ladder I only saw him from above; if I went halfway up I only saw his stomach.

In any case he had such a wide gaping mouth, he ate everything, maybe even me if I came too close. Eventually I realised that from a long way off I could see all of him but then he was no longer a giant.

He aroused my curiosity and I wanted to get to know him so I tried by degrees to get closer to him.

If I'm honest I have to say I was scared but I really wanted to and I was very curious, if only it weren't for that wide wide mouth.

I took my courage in both hands and decided to go up close to him and say that I wasn't edible.

Who knows if he'd have believed me.

Anyway, even if he was so big, I hoped to create some kind of understanding between us.

Certainly seeing him like that…it was awe-inspiring!

I got as far as his feet and in a hoarse voice called to him.

After a while he looked at me.

"Now he's going to eat me," I thought feeling trapped.

I heard myself saying that I wanted to have a good relationship with him.

"Aren't you afraid of me?" he asked. "I'm big, I can stamp on you; one of my movements could create a draught that would knock you down. You know, for this and other reasons I don't have many friends," he confided.

"Don't you worry," I replied. "I shall watch out for your great feet. I shall watch how you open your mouth so that I don't get sucked in – that's my job. I really want to be friends with you. I want to get to know you and I want you to tell me everything about you, what you see from up there and what your body feels as it moves and walks on this earth."

Even if he was big and I small, such was our desire to be together that from that moment on the giant and I became one and the same thing.

PIERINA
GIOVANNA AND THE WITCH GIACINTA
FRANCESCO
CLARETTA GOES TO SCHOOL
ELIA THE LITTLE MONKEY
MY BEST FRIEND
MARIA ROSA
ONE PATH AND MANY KEYS
THE TIMID SUN

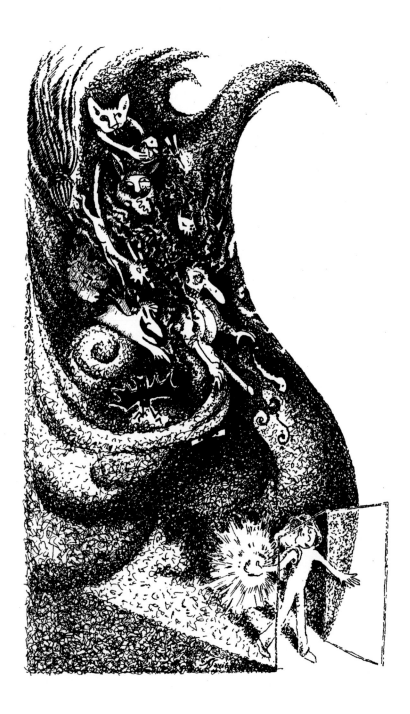

PIERINA

She travelled from one planet to another, small and tucked up in her space-ship.

Her name was Pierina and she was looking for a world to stay in.

You couldn't tell Pierina's age from her face and her body had no traces of the life she had lived. She seemed timeless, even though she displayed that curiosity which gave a sensation of youth.

One particular day she found herself in the garden of Carlo, the Elf, always in a hurry.

"I'm in a rush, a rush, a terrible rush…"

Pierina watched amazed as this creature ran around frenetically from one side of the garden to the other.

While she waited for him to stop, she sat down on the lawn and laid her head on its soft welcoming cushion of daisies which enfolded her in a delicate perfume.

Pierina stopped watching the elf to look up at the sky which she had flown through so many times; she counted the clouds, tasted the warmth of the sun on her face and let her eyes wander freely in the immensity of that limitless blue.

At that moment she realised that, being always wrapped up in trying to get somewhere, she had never noticed that what had seemed to her just empty space was in fact full of different gradations of light and looking closer she saw that it even took on a shape.

She was still immersed in this experience when Carlo the elf called out to her:

"Hallo, I'm Carlo, I didn't say hallo before because I was in such a hurry! You know, I've always got so many things to do that if I don't rush I feel as if I'll never get them done. Oh, how I wish I had a moment to stop and relax like you! By the way, what's your name? And what are you doing here?"

"My name's Pierina and I was looking for the same thing as you but I've found it now."

But already Carlo wasn't listening and had run off to do something else, looking for a place to be.

"Goodbye;" said Pierina. "I hope you find that moment, the one in which you won't have anything to do, as you said. Don't you realise you're spending your life running from one thing to another? You rush through your moments so quickly you don't realise you've had them."

GIOVANNA AND THE WITCH GIACINTA

For a while now Giovanna had had the feeling that there was someone with her. It had all begun one morning when, at her usual time, she had been meditating, listening to the morning's voices and awakenings.

Out of the blue an old woman's face appeared, which she immediately thought of as being that of a witch, in fact it wasn't just one face, it seemed like many. An old woman with straight, wild hair – long and white. Her expression was stern and her eyes were sombre. At the time Giovanna didn't pay much attention but as the day wore on the memory of that morning's experience came back to her. After a few days there was the face again, a second time. And so on, it kept coming back more frequently.

Giovanna had the impression that it was all the fruit of her imagination. She felt more and more upset. She asked herself who the woman might or might not be; she tried to banish her but felt her presence even more.

She tried to give the witch a voice. She could see the red fleshy mouth moving and saying a whole lot of indecipherable things.

When she kept silent the witch was full of an energy which Giovanna had the feeling was inside herself and she was scared. On these occasions she would try breathing deeply and for a while the witch would vanish, only to return.

By now she felt the witch was always with her and bit by

bit she resigned herself to it. When she appeared Giovanna would greet her, saying that all was well, that she could stay if she really wished. She called the witch Giacinta.

"But why are you so ugly?" she had the courage to ask.

Giacinta had by now become a complete figure with a body: A shrivelled up grumpy old woman who wandered about the house.

"I want to draw your portrait," said Giovanna one day.

"No, no, leave me alone," replied Giacinta.

"Go on, just for fun, you know that I enjoyed drawing once."

"All right, if you insist."

"But don't put on a pose like that, hand on hip."

"Well," replied Giacinta, "Whether you like it or not I'm old and ugly. *And* you call me a witch."

"In fact you are a bit scary, with no teeth, that hairy nose, and always sneering – you're not exactly a picture of beauty."

"Bah!..." grumbled Giacinta.

So Giovanna got some paper and drew her portrait. She began to draw and out came a young face with two terrifying eyes. And the more she tried to draw the old woman, the more her pencil drew a young face.

She drew one, two, three, four of them...gradually the eyes got softer.

With the first face Giovanna had been afraid of what she had drawn but she had gone on because she really did want to get Giacinta's likeness. The fourth showed Giacinta when she was young. "But what can it mean?" she asked herself. This face was soft and sweet, almost submissive, like the expression Giovanna remembered in a photo of herself when she was young: a young doe, wounded and resigned to her fate.

She was determined to continue until, having got to the seventh face there was Giacinta just as she had wanted – Giacinta as a child, Giovanna as a child: Giacinta had been concealing a little girl, concealing Giovanna. That's why she grumbled as she shuffled here and there. She had made herself known to Giovanna to refresh her memory, to make her remember the child in her – the child that she had hidden a long time ago to protect her from the world and whom she seemed to have forgotten.

"Thank you, Giacinta; thank you, I'm glad to have known fear: it was me behind you, me Giovanna. Please, Giacinta come whenever I treat myself badly, come whenever I want to hide from myself, come when you think it necessary."

In her subconscious Giovanna realised that she was both young and mature, knowledge and wisdom.

"Goodbye, Giovanna."

FRANCESCO

Maybe you've known someone like Francesco, someone whose qualities distinguished him from other people. He was a likeable young kid, I used to play with him. He was a very unique character. He wore thick glasses and was for ever sneezing. His pockets were always bulging with hand-kerchiefs.

He couldn't stand fog and when it was misty he would stay at home if he could.

"I can't see anything, this fog is suffocating me! I can't see where to put my feet, everything is so nebulous, so unsafe," he complained.

The other children teased him, chanting: "Scaredy, scaredy!"

So he withdrew inside himself and kept away from other people.

When the sun was shining and the air was clear with those glasses of his he managed to read and study and see into the depth of things that other people wouldn't notice. He would observe the beauty of a flower. He would tranquilly watch the ants marching along their trails and patiently follow the flight of birds. He never got tired of watching. He would talk to other people about his impressions and the things he'd observed and at those times he would gather interested listeners around him.

But fog scared him and made him ill at ease since he could

no longer see properly, so he would get upset and feel sad and melancholy.

I've probably already told you that Francesco was full of curiosity, that he read a lot and that he passed the time at home getting to know many things. Just as in good weather he loved to observe the flowers, butterflies and other marvels of nature so he would also immerse himself in his books, fascinated by everything. One day, by chance, looking at some illustrations in a book, he discovered that natural phenomena, like fog, were really interesting.

Certainly it could be annoying, like not being able to see very far. But it only covered things over, it didn't make them disappear! And in any case, maybe on those occasions there was a good chance to look better at the things close to us.

From that day on Francesco took all the different changes in nature in his stride.

When it rained, when it was foggy!

A great opportunity to snuggle up and listen and observe the things right next to you. Near and mysterious.

And there were so many...

Goodbye, Francesco.

CLARETTA GOES TO SCHOOL

It was her first day at school. Claretta went off with her backpack and lunch-basket full of fruit and fresh bread.

She started out happily, her mother had shown her how to get there. She met other children in their brand-new school pinafores, in their eyes the emotion of the first day – curiosity and uncertainty.

They arrived in front of a big school but Claretta waved to her friends and went on.

"Claretta, where are you going, why don't you stop?" asked one of the children.

"I'm going a bit further on, I'm going to another school," replied Claretta.

As she walked she met other children, she said hallo to them and then they went their separate ways.

"But where's Claretta going?" they asked themselves.

Everyday it was the same thing.

"Claretta why don't you come with us to your proper school?" they asked, trying to insist.

Finally Claretta replied:

"Because Mummy has chosen a special school for me."

Then she explained.

"In the school I go to the walls are all coloured. The benches are huge carpets where you can sit and hold hands. There are tables for writing and drawing. We study maths by counting flower petals. We make friends with the animals. We observe nature in its real habitat and you always discover something new. We study anatomy making friends with our bodies. We learn history getting to know our ancient land and how to look after it.

We get our bearings by knowing that North is where the pole-star is. We study the stars and that big star, the sun; the cycle of the seasons and fruits it offers us; the fields and how the corn grows. Many, many things, never ending. So you see, we learn lots of useful things."

"Oh!..." exclaimed one child, "But why ever did your mother send you to that school?"

"Because she loves me," replied Claretta.

ELIA THE LITTLE MONKEY

Elia lived in the big forest with a band of monkeys and moved around with them as they looked for food. In the life of the group she had her own duties and she was happy like that but she had a problem about which she didn't know what to do. Everyone knows that monkeys climb trees, they practically live there, jumping from branch to branch with amazing skill. Well, Elia was afraid of heights, she didn't climb much and stayed on the lower branches, always apprehensive. She was used to living with this problem but she knew she had to and could solve it by herself. Her companions were no trouble, apart from the occasional one who would tease her but she didn't care.

She lived with this fear and, even if sometimes she was tempted to climb a bit further up a tree, she always put it off for lack of courage.

"It's not the end of the world if I don't go further up," Elia would say but whenever she stopped and looked around her eyes would always travel upwards and she would sigh.

At a certain point a situation presented itself that Elia couldn't avoid.

"Fair enough, I've put it off for so long and hoped for something to happen. Now I've got to act and come to think of it, I'm glad."

That day she and her companions found themselves in front of a group of very tall tree and there were no small ones for miles. They were running away because they were being chased and didn't want to end up as someone's dinner, so they started to climb. Elia did likewise and climbed and climbed. She got cold sweats but she went on up until she got to the first branch. It was really high and this time looking down she thought it was the end for her.

She stayed a long time clinging to the trunk, not having the courage to move. Her thoughts exploded in a succession of fears until her mind totally emptied out and she started to feel the contact of her body with the tree. The rough, fresh bark gave out an aromatic smell. She started to move her fingers and discovered that the grooves in the bark could serve as handholds. She moved her limbs as well and found that she could not only hold onto the tree but climb as well – as in fact she had already done – and she began to feel more secure.

Gradually she tried moving and sat herself comfortably on the branch. At first she looked in front of her, then all around. How beautiful it was up there!

Now she could feel the trees as her friend and bit by bit started to trust its strength. She felt its solidity, how firmly it was planted and that she could stay there as long as she wanted.

"I can always go down in the same way I came up," she reassured herself and finally looked down.

Her head spun a little.

"It's because I'm seeing things from another angle but seeing them like that doesn't mean that I'm stranded. I got here by climbing up and I'll get down by climbing down. Certainly from up here the view is marvellous and different!" Elia told herself.

Finally she started climbing down and realised that her long arms could reach out for the branches further away.

"How good it is to have got started! I'd like to try out everything and jump from branch to branch but I'd better stop at this now."

Elia was more than satisfied with her day, in fact quite moved by her experience. "Try things out, do a little at a time," she reflected. "I want to taste everything, novelties – all the never-ending discoveries that will give spice to my life and which I finally feel like making."

That evening Elia went to sleep happy and when she woke up in the morning she no longer had that anguish that had accompanied her and hindered her from realising her wishes.

MY BEST FRIEND

When I first met her I was so young that I can't recall exactly how old I was.

Like me, as a little girl, she had grown up in a convent school where life on the surface seemed to be the same for everyone, even though deep in our hearts each one of us kept many secrets. She liked to live in that sort of mystery. The daily routine left no traces of diversity between the children. Everyone had to be good, well-behaved, exemplary...it was really a very strict and severe school. There weren't many of us, maybe no more than twenty, but to me it seemed hundreds.

In the silence between us, looks, gestures or movements created ways of communicating that the adults couldn't decipher – the important thing was that one lived within the established patterns without disturbing them.

We all quickly learned these arts but I remember that she suffered in particular.

Sometimes happy and lively but more often than not sad, she couldn't find a way of relating easily to other girls.

Not until she was nine years old did she have the opportunity to meet her parents; when she met her mother, that wasn't a very pleasant experience for her, a person she knew absolutely nothing about.

Religion, the main subject at school, had a considerable influence on her personality. Hell, Purgatory, Heaven: these were awesome things to fear and respect. Likewise what they called "Mystery" – which she accepted humbly and passively.

But apart from this she had every intention of getting to know everything. She studied and read; she had a good voice and was in the choir. Her secret wish was to play the piano and be a dancer. She loved drawing and adored nature. At that time she was always writing poetry, naturally this was kept firmly hidden: you had to stay absolutely within the accepted rules.

If you wanted or dreamed of something different that meant lack of humility.

I remember that although she tried very hard to be good, her mind would follow its own paths. She did manage to talk to me and to see and work things out for herself.

She suffered a great deal from lack of affection but even if her needs often came to the fore, she accepted her surroundings and tried to adapt.

I remember enough things about her to write a book. For instance, her adolescence, her first love affair and the effect on her when at fourteen years old she left school and faced a totally unknown world.

I know that life for her slid past in a series of more or less difficult and unacceptable experiences and adventures. She was always on the look-out for that hidden something.

She lived more through her surroundings than through herself just as she had been taught.

For a long time I didn't see her. A dense mist had formed between us. We kept in touch for years and she told me she was still searching and suffering.

At a certain point, many years ago, I decided I would never see her again. She made me feel too sad, too desperate. I remembered her only with her problems and difficulties.

Inside me I still have that fear of meeting her, of facing her expression, her eyes, not knowing how to react. Seeing her again, seeing her body, her face, her hair, what effect would it have on me and what would I say? Would she have stayed as she was then?

That very child, that very girl! What if she were different now? Seeing her, I would have to throw away that part of her which had stuck in my memory and which for all this time I'd tried not to meet.

This morning I went for a drive. Those places I knew so well, which had lately been upsetting me so much, are still there. At a certain point I recognised old smells, a familiar atmosphere. "Yes, I recognise you," I said to myself, "but I can't make you disappear just by pretending not to see you. It's not by putting on dark glasses that I'll ever avoid you, or not remember you. It's fine to want to get away from here, to be elsewhere but to not leave you the way I tried to."

My dear childhood friend and the places of my past – you are things to be taken by the hand, stroked, say goodbye to, and leave "with Love."

MARIA ROSA

Maria Rosa was someone who never liked what she was wearing. She had a wardrobe packed with beautiful clothes. She had started work recently but her parents continued to make sure she lacked for nothing: her mother still helped her buy her clothes, so she was never free to choose for herself.

Everyone liked her. Her parents liked her, her friends liked her but she didn't like herself: her clothes were too tight for her.

"Lucky you, with a figure that looks good in everything," her friends said. But she suffered, because every time she closed the zip she had to hold her breath; her dresses squeezed her and often upset her digestion. Sometimes she tried to explain but would get the reply:

"Darling, you look so good, you really make an impression – it's great going out with you, you have such a slim figure!"

"How is it possible that no-one notices that I'm suffering inside these clothes, which are admittedly beautiful but too small? How can they not see, not realise? It seems to me I'm walking stiffly and awkwardly, I can hardly breathe and they say I'm pretty!"

Shut up in her room she brooded more and more about it, until one day she went out, and came back with a dress bought and chosen by her alone. She went up to her room and tried it on.

"Ah...how good I feel!" exclaimed Maria Rosa.

She looked in the mirror. Her figure was soft, the curves had a roundness she had not really understood before. She liked herself like that and she saw that there was something attractive about her. It felt good – at least she could breathe and she felt lighter, more relaxed. Finally she could move freely.

"Not showing the real me made me feel heavy, while now looking in the mirror I see myself as I really am," thought Maria Rosa and slowly, calmly, she left her room to go and show herself to her parents, her friends, everyone who knew her.

"Thank you for all that you have done for me to make me look good to the rest of the world but from now on I'm going to let you off this task. I assure you I shall take responsibility for who I am and how I look. I apologise in advance if at times I might not please you as much but that doesn't mean I love you any less."

With a loving look for them all, she went away. Even if her figure was not so slim and slender, inside herself she felt light and happy.

ONE PATH AND MANY KEYS

One day Chiara went to the Fair, where she found a very special merry-go-round. Her curiosity was aroused and she asked what it was. They told her that it offered different ways of playing the game. The merry-go-round was in fact a big park with tunnels, underground passages, various gates and many paths. At the start she would be given a bunch of keys. Choosing whatever path she felt like, she could finish up either at the exit marked "Satisfaction" or the one marked "Dissatisfaction". From this second exit however, she could, if she still had the energy, turn back and go on looking for the other.

Chiara decided to try and bought her ticket.

She set off on a track that led after a bit to a big crossroads with many paths leading off.

"Which to choose?" she asked herself and took one at random.

As she went along she found a gate, opened it using one of the keys from her bunch and continued on her way. Further on the path merged with another and she happily took this one.

She walked for a long while without noticing the time passing, just looking around. The route, always the same, an unmade track that wandered through the greenery. Quite soon she found herself at the exit but she wasn't at all satisfied, the journey had been pretty monotonous. She'd had a nice walk but she thought she would try some different experiences, so she went back to the crossroads and took another path.

This one was also unmade. It led through a tunnel and at various times she had to open gates in order to continue. At a certain point the path became dark and went inside a huge underground passage. Chiara was frightened but her curiosity drew her on.

She came to a jet-black gate and searched for the right key. beyond the tunnel opened out, its walls covered in branches with flowers of every hue. Immediately afterwards she found another gate, green this time. She opened it: there was a fountain of the clearest water which Chiara could drink from and see herself in it. Going on she discovered a third gate, brown and massive. Patiently she extracted the key to this one also and on opening it found herself in a warm welcoming room with an open fire. There was a table laid out with food and Chiara sat down to eat.

Further on there was a blue iron gate, behind which a flock of bright birds were singing sweetly. Then she found a great door of many colours, leading on to a room whose walls had projected onto them all the images of all the paths Chiara had followed.

She was very satisfied with the choice she had made; to have tried opening all those gates and doors; to have seen so many marvellous things. Now she wasn't sure whether to go on or turn back to the first path which would take her easily to the exit.

She looked at the bunch of keys. She knew she still had many untried ones so she continued along the path with the many gates but which had only one exit.

Her happiness was complete because she had understood that she could open doors and find a part of herself behind each of them.

65

THE TIMID SUN

They told him that the sun burns, that it parches the earth and that he was the child of a sun he had never known.

In the morning as soon as he woke up he looked for something to hide behind as he was very shy. With envy and jealousy he watched his friends the clouds going about happily in the sky. At times the wind separated them or merged them one with the other but they weren't worried – they accepted it, in fact for them it was a game, they enjoyed it.

He asked the nearest cloud:

"Would you mind hiding me today as well?"

He always found one of them happy to help him but every now and then it happened that they all blew far away at once.

The sky then became clear and the sun rushed at once to hide behind a mountain.

Sometimes he would wake up where there were no mountains, not even a hill. Desperately he would look for refuge behind the first tree, adapting his shape. He would stretch out long, pull himself in and shrink to hide as best he could.

It was a great effort and he would wake up crushed and full of bumps. He was no longer beautifully round but all dented, with swellings here and there from his strained and forced postures.

He had lost all his elasticity and found it more and more difficult to hide and change his shape behind things.

One morning when he opened his eyes he found himself in the middle of a clear sky with the sea below him. There was no high ground, no tree, no cloud to hide behind and panic overtook him.

What could he do?

He knew by now that the earth spins on its own axis and that every morning when he woke he would find himself in a different place.

Now in front of him was the void, the ocean. It could equally have been the desert and he knew that sooner or later he would have found himself in this situation but he'd always hoped that it wouldn't happen.

He stayed stock still from fear, and looked about him.

Something luminous was shining around him. Its farthest points, like rays, were making a warm play of light on the sky. His curiosity aroused, he dared to look further down towards the earth and saw himself reflected in the sea. He was beautiful: orange, red and yellow. His light transformed all the colours in the water.

He started making movements, playing, observing his golden reflections on the surface or in the depths of the sea.

Enchanted, he gradually began to relax.

He saw how all around him it was brighter and everything, as far as his rays reached, opened itself up.

Over there far away, flower petals were unfolding; men were throwing wide their windows to let the warmth in; children's smiles were expanding in radiant, joyous moments of happiness; lizards were stretching themselves and animals were coming out of their dens.

He was happy.

"But where have I been all this time?" he asked himself. "I was shy, I was insecure. Goodness knows what I was thinking of, what I believed!...when all that was needed was to be myself."

The sun realised that at last he could start living an entirely different life: new, his own, without hiding-places and above all without rigid patterns.

MARINELLA
TERESINA THE SPIDER
THE COLOURED BALLOON
ANNA
GINO THE ELF
ROBERTO THE GLOBETROTTER
THE MAGIC CASKET
ELISA THE LITTLE ANT
THE ANGEL CALLED CHATTERBOX

MARINELLA

She had red hair and masses of freckles. Her shining eyes in a round face gave the impression of a ripe fruit. She had been given the name of Marinella because her cheeks were always so red. Children said that her face looked like a cherry.

Marinella was a lively and happy child; everyone in the village liked her. When she passed along the street all the colours became brighter and she infected everyone she met with her vitality and lightheartedness.

She was very imaginative and often played with the long coloured ribbons that her mother had found in the attic. She didn't know whose they had been, whether her grandmother's or great grandmother's.

Marinella loved them and whenever she could she invented games with them.

She loved running through the meadows holding them by one end so that they formed trails of coloured spirals in the air. She imagined they were rainbows and delighted in the wavy movements that the wind created as it caressed them.

Sometimes she chose a particular one whose colour she liked and twined it round a chair a tree or other things.

One day a circus arrived in the village square. It had wonderful conjurers and jugglers. Marinella, like all the other children, couldn't wait to go. On the day of the show, in the afternoon, after having said goodbye to her parents, she set off with her long ribbons down the road that lead to the centre of the village.

She was excited and very curious then she saw a man coming towards her who didn't look very reassuring.

Marinella slowed down and the man immediately came closer:

"What lovely ribbons!" he exclaimed.

"Well, yes…" replied Marinella.

The man started zigzagging as if to stop her continuing on her way.

"You're really fortunate to have those ribbons. I would really like you to lend them to me just for today. I work for the circus, you know, and they would be very important."

Marinella, taken aback, tried to understand what he was saying. The man went on:

"I'm a quick-change artist and with your ribbons I could make a different appearance for every colour" and he began to sob. Then he continued: "I was very good once but bit by bit I lost my inventiveness. If I don't do my number today at the circus they'll fire me and I'll have no work!"

"Oh well… if that's how things stand… I could lend them to you for today, only today mind. I'll come with you, I was going to the circus myself. You'll find me there afterwards and you can give them back to me."

"Thank you, beautiful child" and with a rapid movement pulling the ribbons from Marinella's hands, he disappeared equally quickly.

Marinella swallowed hard; her legs were by no means steady, her normal calm was disturbed and all her cheerfulness had suddenly vanished.

She got to the circus and sat right in the front row. When the show began she searched ever more anxiously for the quick-change artist.

At a certain point he appeared, wrapped in a blaze of ribbons. Everyone sat bolt upright with astonishment: his face kept changing form and showing them different characteristics. The ribbons wound round the man in a huge spiral of shimmering colours and tones.

After the initial amazement, there was a burst of applause. Marinella couldn't move – she felt threatened, in danger and miserable as if she had been robbed of something.

Her intuition began to glimpse a truth she didn't want to accept.

After a time the light emanating from the ribbons began to fade and she saw more and more clearly the figure of a man who, unlike the one she had seen in the road, had a face with flaming eyes and a body bursting with vitality.

Turning directly to Marinella, he said: "I've been looking for a long time for someone like you who possessed all the colours of life, because I desperately needed them. I no longer had any energy, but now, stealing it from you, I feel reinvigorated." At these words he vanished, leaving the young girl stunned, unable to believe what had happened.

With difficulty Marinella dragged herself home where her understanding parents tried to console her but without her ribbons she felt lost.

The colour started to drain from her face, the sparkle went out of her eyes – it was as if that man had carried away her enthusiasm for life. She couldn't understand how these things could have been taken from her.

Nothing interested her anymore and she stayed shut up in the house. She often went back to the attic to look nostalgically at the trunk where her mother had found the ribbons...then one day she opened it. She delicately moved aside all the things that it held and underneath, right at the bottom, she found a box of coloured crayons. Opening it, a sheet of paper slid out which Marinella hastened to read with curiosity:

"Many colours for drawing many spirals of light; for drawing rainbows, for drawing ribbon bows, for colouring gusts of wind, for colouring your moods.

Colours for the brown of your eyes, the pink of your cheeks, for a blue sky when it's raining; and red for a heart as big as the world, which will give your life energy just like coloured ribbons."

{"Marinella" is a dialect name used in the Veneto region for a type of maraschino cherry. *Translator's note.*}

TERESINA THE SPIDER

She was ugly, she was purple, she was Teresina the Spider: oval and hairy with three eyes and many many legs. And she had an enormous, horrible mouth.

When she moved around she always had her little baby purple spiders with her. They kept close to her in ranks like soldiers. Teresina's hair was long and when she stayed still it swayed like grass in the wind.

Her legs were in continuous motion, weaving, weaving miles of webs. Her babies were always twitching their legs as well.

Once she was on the move, she would go on for ages, never stopping, so much so that it was quite a shock when she did stay still, it was so rare. Then she would look at you with two wicked eyes while she kept the third closed and laughed mockingly. She gave the impression of working out some diabolical plan.

It was exhausting – even when she was asleep she looked wide awake. She made such thick webs that if any little animal tried to walk or fly past it became instantly imprisoned or literally swallowed up by her mouth.

The babies, little monsters, copied their mother so that the web became an impregnable fortress.

Teresina had by now managed to block a very important path so the little animals of the village arranged a meeting to find a solution.

Various strategies were proposed but not one of them seemed to work. Attacking her only aggravated the beast. So in the end they unanimously agreed to look for another path.

Giorgio the owl, who could see at night, started tirelessly flying over the area until finally, as he was following the stream, he realised its possibilities as a new route. The stream flowed downhill so they decided to construct some boats to make use of the current.

For a while this solution worked well but when the stream was swollen with the rains it became difficult to navigate. So they arranged another meeting and as they talked they realised the necessity of reopening the path where Teresina was.

But how? Both ways were very important. Just using the stream wasn't enough. Giorgio, the wise owl, took a message to Teresina asking for her help as the village really needed her. At first the little spider couldn't care less, in fact she relished the situation, but when nobody ever came near her anymore she started to feel lonely.

She decided to let go her hold and one by one she undid her webs.

With her babies she gradually cleared the path and as a little bit of light began showing through from the other side: an intense perfume of roses also wafted through. By degrees a rose garden appeared which Teresina had jealously kept hidden because she didn't want any animal going into it. She was afraid that one of them might ruin it for her since she'd had that kind of experience in the past. Next to the path some big moles had invaded that wonderful garden of hers so to protect it she had constructed a wall of webs in a complete circle.

"Like that I can feel safe," she had said.

She had instructed her little ones to do the same. They had got on with it and obeyed, even if they didn't understand why.

Teresina started to put blades of grass in her hair and decorate her body with daisy petals. Her appearance became much softer and the animals started to regard her amicably as they passed unmolested along the path.

If there was a party in the village Teresina brought a bunch of roses, her most beautiful ones. In this way there grew up a good relationship of friendship, not only between Teresina and the inhabitants of the village but also between her and all the passers-by who, as they arrived, would smell the scent of the roses.

Teresina gave a rose to anyone who wanted.

The others? They could only smell the perfume.

THE COLOURED BALLOON

One evening my son and I were lying in bed when, at a certain point, he announced that he felt sad. I reassured him that I was right there looking after him.

After a bit he said again that he was sad. He was sleepy but the sadness stopped him from sleeping.

I thought calmly and made a small request to God for help and the answer came to me.

"Close your eyes and imagine you have a balloon which You're holding by its string. What colour is it?" I asked.

"Red," he replied.

"Now let's write the word *Sadness* on it and let go the string slowly so it flies away."

"It's vanished into the sky," said my son and then began again: "Now there's a yellow balloon."

"Good, we can write *Joy* on it."

"Now there's an orange one."

"*Happiness*," I replied.

"A blue one."

"*Serenity*."

"A green one."

"*Meadows*."

"And brown?" he asked me in another, almost worried voice.

"*Wood*, like tree-trunks with their scented resin."

"Grey?"

"*Rain*, in fact there are drops on the balloon if you look carefully."

"White?"

"Let's see, turning it round and round I'm starting to read *Light*. It looks like a light-bulb this balloon", and by now I was worried I wouldn't find any more answers.

"Black?"

Calmly I replied:

"*Night* and in fact the word is written in yellow and it's as bright as the stars."

"Violet?" his voice became more and more subdued.

"*Cloud*, as in the colours of the sunset." "Certainly," I added, "looking at these coloured balloons spinning around is really nice – and finding out what's written on them. They're so light up there in the sky, aren't they?"

"Mmm…" was all the reply I got.

My son was happily going to sleep.

ANNA

A while ago I met Anna, a very likeable girl, full of ideas and enthusiasm. I remember she always had masses to do; she would start lots of things and sometimes not finish them.

I'll admit I didn't find it easy to be with her, since I never knew what mood she'd be in, but she was so full of life that it was impossible not to seek out her company.

Whenever I went to see her she would take me to her room which was packed with things. Every object represented an event from her past and she was so good at telling you about them in all their detail that it was like hearing fairy stories. I never knew if she was adding bits from her imagination, her past was so rich!

I would go away happy. I always learned something or rather I felt she had given me something helpful which made me feel good.

But when she was sad she really suffered; behind her eyes were limitless dark and stormy seas. All at once I would see the mist descend over her face and it was if she had disappeared.

"Where are you?" I would ask.

"I am where pain, fear, sadness and death are," Anna would reply and suddenly I would feel icy. It might seem strange but I never managed to accept this state of hers and wanted to help her to do something, but I didn't know what. Then after some time, maybe, I would find her so happy as to seem the most carefree person in the world, until one day she confided in me: "You know, I've made a journey to the inside of fear."

I didn't understand what she meant but tried to listen attentively.

"It's a vast place, you can lose yourself in it," she continued. "Inside there is everything that can do harm" and she took my hands in hers. She looked around and glanced at all her things. Then she went on:

"You know I never really liked all these things and didn't know why I hung on to them. I suppose at least I gave them some kind of importance by keeping them stuck in my memory. I didn't realise that by doing that I wasn't allowing space for anything new or other ways of living.

"Those things represent moments of my past experiences characterised by lack of understanding – even products of circumstance – whereas my real needs stayed inside me, hidden, buried. I've often looked angrily at these objects thinking how I would like to have lived differently.

"Now here I am in this place, in the present, and the Anna-of-now is still doing the same thing and reacting to what she sees according to the habits she's learned.

"At that time I was young, I didn't have any guide but now I'm grown up and I realise how important it is to live for what you are with the richness of what you have been.

"At last the hold that that way of living – only sticking to what I knew – had on me, is no longer strong enough to harm me. Now you understand the reason for my conflicts and my bad moods."

I looked at Anna with tears in my eyes. I'd never heard anyone talk so frankly before, opening herself up totally in front of another person. Therefore, I said:

"I assure you that time has not taken anything from you."

"Thank you," she replied. "I want so much to live and I'm still learning…what I was, what I'd like to be…I'm learning to live how I actually am."

She got up off the bed where she'd been sitting and started taking all the things out of the room. In the end there was just the furniture.

"How bare it is!" said Anna, a bit bewildered.

"It's not bare: because you're here," I replied and we hugged each other.

GINO THE ELF

He lived down there, where the woods finish and a wide valley opens out.

His name was Gino and he was an elf.

You couldn't see his house but everyone knew it was somewhere around there.

Let me explain: Gino had made himself a very strange house, built underground, so you went in from on top, by the roof. You should know that many years ago Gino was known as a somewhat extravagant person and rather interfering. He would talk to everybody, making a great deal of noise and never keeping still. They often said that he should learn to keep himself in check and not be so overpowering.

For a little while Gino would put the brakes on but then at the least expected times his nature would burst out again. Then it was a disaster. Practically everyone avoided him and eventually he found himself alone.

He decided to disappear and built himself his underground house. He dug out an enormous amount, enough to make it huge with lots of rooms, so that he could build his whole world in there and no-one could criticise him any more.

Walking along the bottom of the valley you could see in the grass a little chimney close to a hatch, always locked from the inside. The air would come in through the chimney and sometimes even faint scents of nature.

He had even worked out a system of artificial lighting so as not to be in the dark.

Everything he possessed was in that underground house.

He thought he was isolated from the world but he was wrong, because even under the ground as we know there are inhabitants, some familiar, some less so. Sometimes he heard sounds but couldn't work out where they were coming from. His curiosity aroused, he set himself patiently to listen.

From the other side of the wall, always at the same time of day, he could hear someone crying. One day he beat on the wall but got no response. So he made all the noise he possibly could and at last he heard a signal from the other side.

"Please go on making your noise," said a voice.

"Who are you?" asked the elf.

"I'm a strange being or rather I don't remember who I am, whether I'm tall or short, male or female, young or old."

"But how is that possible?" asked Gino.

"It's been a long time or perhaps not. I'm a 'Don't Know.'"

"A Don't Know?"

Gino was totally baffled.

"Please talk," asked the voice, "go on talking, talking about anything, I've only got you."

"All right," replied Gino and wetting his lips he started to talk, tell stories, make music and sing. Every now and then, exhausted, he would stop and fall into a deep sleep.

The voice called to him begging him to go on making himself heard. Gino felt that he was talking a whole lot of nonsense by this time but the voice said that wasn't important and would he please go on. He talked for ever, played his music, clapped his hands, jumped up and down, did everything in fact and even more but the voice went on asking him to continue.

"I don't know, at this point I really don't know what else to do," he said quite desperate.

"I beg you. Don't Know, that's me – just go on doing anything you want, otherwise I'll die."

Gino looked around him: he'd done everything. He'd turned the house upside down, moved the furniture, anything to make every conceivable type of noise.

"What on earth can I do now?" he asked himself.

He could do something else, he realised now. So he opened the hatch.

"Don't Know, do you notice the sound of the wind, of the rain…the heat of the sun?"

"What are they?"

"It's useless trying to explain – Don't Know needs to feel, to see," thought Gino. He took his pick and started breaking up the ceiling to make a hole, knocking down the walls and the roof, letting in the light of Nature with all its sounds.

Then he went right out into the open.

"Don't Know, breathe!" encouraged Gino. "Sniff, listen, come out, don't stay shut up in there!"

In the meantime he realised that Don't Know had already got out. He'd gone.

They tell me that now there is a beautiful house at the end of the valley.

ROBERTO THE GLOBETROTTER

Roberto was an ageless man and, although his appearance was youthful, no-one had any idea how old he was. People knew that he loved to travel the world and that at one time he had been a teacher. Now however he organised unusual and amusing activities such as setting up a puppet theatre or playing the clown in the town square riding a unicycle. In other words he liked entertaining people and seeing new places.

One day he came upon a beautiful village. The houses were small and white. All around were trees laden with fruit, vineyards, corn-fields as far as the eye could see and flowers everywhere.

It always made him happy when he found such a beautiful place on his travels.

He was going along the white stony road that led to the centre of the village, singing contentedly, when he met an old man walking bent double under the weight of a sack that seemed very heavy. Roberto stopped a moment and asked if he wanted some help but the old man said no and went on his way.

The further he got towards the heart of the village the more people he met carrying sacks on their shoulders. They all walked somewhat bent, even the children had a little sack tied behind their backs and were playing games with their sacks.

Roberto stopped at a certain point and sat down perplexed on a bench to observe this strange phenomenon. There was not one person who was not bent under the weight of a sack.

He went up to another man, no longer very young and asked him why they were going around like that.

"What, don't you know? For us it's normal, what's so strange about it? It's a custom of ours and for that matter why don't you do it?"

Roberto replied that he had never followed such a custom, and that he probably would have found it highly awkward. Curious, he inquired:

"But what have you got in there?"

"That's where we store our past. We can't leave it lying around and what if we lost it?"

At this Roberto asked:

"But to what end? What do you do with it? Don't you feel hampered in your movements?"

"Who knows?" replied the old man. "I don't know what you're talking about, it's a tradition of ours."

Roberto looked around and noted that the fruit trees were full of fruit at the top and empty underneath. The houses were small and low with nicely painted walls but badly maintained roofs. After a certain height practically everything was different. He sought an explanation from the old man about this observation, who told him:

"You see, the young people, who are normally lighter, get up to a certain height, they can climb up but then as the years go by the sack gets heavier from all their various experiences and so…"

"You seem fairly resigned to the matter," observed Roberto.

"You know sometimes I'd like to take off my sack, but I don't know, it seems safer with all one's stock of experiences on one's back. That's what I learned and that's how we live in this village, I really couldn't say…"

"But have you once, just once, tried to lighten it, to get rid of what you no longer need?" said Roberto and so saying he pretended to lose his balance and knocked into the old man, who's sack slid to the ground.

I should point out that the inhabitants of the village were always careful when they were out walking not to bump into each other and when they got close they held their sacks tight for fear of losing them.

So now the old man found himself with his sack on the ground, all torn and split open. The things were spread all over the place and he looked at them bewildered.

Roberto discretely moved a little way away but the old man called him back and started to laugh and laughed so loud that he attracted attention. Quite a few people came up and saw the old man with tears in his eyes laughing and jumping about. Finally having calmed down he looked around and said in a loud voice:

"I don't need these things any more." Taking Roberto by the arm, he added: "I don't know where you come from but thank you for coming here. From this moment on I've decided to break with tradition and not carry the sack any more. You can stay at my house for a while if that would please you. I'd very much like to get to know you and find out how you live. I see that without the sack your back is nice and straight."

"Thank you," replied Roberto and then added: "You know it's not just here, this custom, you find it in other places as well. I remember hearing about it before. Personally, I don't think it's a good idea to hang on to experiences if they become a burden to yourself and others" and after a pause: "I love children very much and I try to learn from them: they are great teachers."

"But what kind of work do you do?"

"Parent, teacher, what does it matter? I'm a man like plenty of others, who meets many people, gets to know different customs and makes his choice."

The old man asked:

"What do you like doing in life?"

"Many things but especially not filling children's sacks."

THE MAGIC CASKET

When she was born Mary had received a gift from her grandmother, a very beautiful casket covered with a quilted sky-blue fabric. Her grandmother told Mary that she could open the casket only when she was twelve years old.

Mary always kept it on the bedside table in her bedroom and couldn't wait to open it.

The years went by and on her twelfth birthday finally Mary went to the casket and, holding her breath from emotion and curiosity, opened it.

At first she gasped with astonishment and backed away dazzled by the light coming from it. Inside were twelve marvellous coloured crystals, each with its own name engraved on a label.

Close to the white crystal was written 'Simplicity'; the yellow one was called 'Smiles', the orange 'Joy', the red 'Love', the pink 'Serenity', the two green ones 'Harmony and Hope', the azure 'Horizons', the blue 'Peace', the brown 'Warmth', the black 'Tears', the violet 'Transformation'.

Mary had never seen anything like it. Fascinated, she reached out her hands to touch the crystals. Each one emanated its own warmth, not one of them was cold and they all gave out a different light. She turned them over in her hands for a long time and then put them back into the casket.

For days she thought about her gift and how unique it

was. Constantly struck by those words written next to the crystals, she pondered on their meaning.

Time passed and every now and then Mary would open the wonderful casket and gaze entranced at the light which came from inside it but then she noticed that some crystals had begun to give off less light and colour. She was a little worried at this and observing them carefully she saw that every evening the ones associated with her own emotions during that day would fade or intensify accordingly.

In the end the crystals and their colours became a kind of account of her life and experiences.

The black one was the one she touched least, for the simple reason that no-one wants to cry and she tried hard to live according to the other colours, thinking that in that way she would always see the crystals shining strongly.

After a while, though, she realised to her dismay that the colours were less vibrant and that by now the black had become dull and the red was fading away.

Mary couldn't understand it, she filled her life with all the beautiful things she could and one evening, with the casket open in her hands, in her desperation she began to weep. As the tears began to wet the crystals, even the black one, she saw that they were starting to shine again.

Then Mary understood that all the colours were necessary in her life. At that precise moment the casket rose up and transformed itself into a cloud, the crystals into coloured confetti which disappeared into the sky.

"Thank you, Granny," said Mary and wept tears of joy.

ELISA, THE LITTLE ANT

Elisa, the little ant, was lively and inquisitive. Outside the ant's nest she would move almost immediately away from the group to wander around in search of adventure and novelty.

One day she came home all excited saying that she'd heard a man talking about some very high mountains, the greatest in the world, the Himalayas and she wanted to know right away where they were in order to go and find them.

"Get all that stuff out of your head," they replied "and stay here where you're safe. It's dangerous to go looking for such huge things!" but Elisa wasn't satisfied and looked elsewhere for the answer.

Along the path she met Gina, the grasshopper, who was always boasting of her long jumps.

"How long are they?" asked Elisa.

"Oh, more than a metre," replied Gina.

"A metre! What's a metre?" thought Elisa and continued on her way.

After a bit she met Lara, the snail and asked what metres were.

"I don't know, I only know about centimetres and millimetres."

"What are they?" But Lara didn't reply.

She stopped under a leaf, bewildered and was asking herself what metres, centimetres and millimetres were, when Tobia the blackbird came sailing down and landed in front of her.

"Tobia, do you know what metres, centimetres and millimetres are?"

"No, I know the heights of the branches from the ground but I have no idea what you are talking about."

"Oh dear, I'll never know," said Elisa discouraged and at that moment she heard the snuffling of Sara the fox, who, after getting her breath back from so much running, told her about kilometres.

By now she knew about lengths but she didn't know what 'greatness' could mean. "So, let's go over it: height, breadth, metres and all that...they are for measuring all sorts of things but greatness, how do you see that, how do you measure that? I've heard that the Himalayas are great mountains – if I see them I'll know what greatness is."

It was already evening and on her way back she met Geremia the owl.

"What's the matter Elisa, you're looking very pensive, is something wrong?"

"You know, Geremia, I've heard about the Himalayas, the biggest mountains in the world and they say they're magnificent but how can I get to see them? I understand how tall they must be but I want to experience their greatness.

To this Geremia replied:

"If you want to understand greatness you don't have to go so far away. You just have to look at the blade of grass in front of you. It is just as magnificent as the Himalayas, just as all-encompassing. This is the measure of greatness.

THE ANGEL CALLED CHATTERBOX

It was a beautiful night. The sky was so clear and deep you could touch the stars with your eyes.

Serena, moved by such beauty, watched and had no thought of going to bed.

"Not for all the gold in the world am I going to miss this splendour," she said out loud.

So taken was she by the solemn and impressive atmosphere that she was not surprised when a voice replied.

She looked down and saw an angel in front of her sitting smiling on a little cloud.

"Glad to meet you Serena! It's actually not always easy to see the immensity of the sky – tonight's a very special night."

"Who are you?"

"I'm the Angel Chatterbox, I'm travelling all over the world, I've got a very important job to do."

Serena forgot the sky and looked with curiosity at the angel who added after a while:

"I'll stop here a bit with you, if you invite me to keep you company."

"I'm rather confused, I don't know what it might be like to keep an angel company."

"Don't you worry, if you like I'll stay here with you just long enough to reveal a secret to you. I'm going from child to child and my job is to tell them where Paradise is."

"Wow!..." exclaimed Serena astonished and with a child's typical sense of humour teased him saying she thought Chatterbox was a very curious name. The angel parked his cloud close to Serena's window, folded his wings, sat down on the windowsill next to her and said:

"You know, when I lived down here on Earth, I took everything very seriously, I thought a great deal, talked a great deal and often forgot that there is such a thing as humour. When I went up there, I met lots of angels who were always laughing their heads off and it was infectious. The more I laughed the lighter I felt and that made my wings sprout. My name is itself a sort of joke so I don't forget to laugh. Considering how important it has always been for me to talk, they gave me this job of coming down to Earth to make contact with the children."

Serena began to feel that it was actually natural and pleasant to be in his company. She closed her eyes and took in this sensation. "Paradise..." she murmured. "Tell me where Paradise is. I'd love to know!"

Chatterbox got up, opened his wings and wrapped the little girl in his pure whiteness. She felt her limbs warm and relaxed and her heart overflowing with life and joy.

"I can feel the beauty of the sky I was watching just now and the intensity of its colours. I can see the light of the stars inside my thoughts, the peacefulness of the night in my heart!" exclaimed Serena, opening her eyes.

The Angel was already on his little cloud ready to go off.

"Now," he said, "you know where Paradise is: inside and outside you. Always see it with the eyes of a child and maybe with a sense of humour too, then we'll get together from time to time to fly around a bit! Goodbye!," and he disappeared into the sky where he had come from.

INDICES

FATHER CHRISTMAS'S PRESENT 9
THE STAR AND THE YOUNG HORSE 10
CHIARA 12
THE ENCHANTED CASTLE 14
HOW SILENCE GAVE ME MY VOICE 16
CARLO THE ACROBAT 18
TALKING TO THE SEA 21
MOTHER LUCIA'S GIFT 25
WHAT IF... 29
MARTA AND THE FABLES 32
THE SOLITARY PRINCESS 33
MASSIMO 37
GETTING TO KNOW AUTUMN 38
THE WONDERFUL CYCLE OF LIFE 41
THE GIANT WITH THE HUGE MOUTH 43
PIERINA 47
GIOVANNA AND THE WITCH GIACINTA 49
FRANCESCO 52
CLARETTA GOES TO SCHOOL 54
ELIA THE LITTLE MONKEY 56
MY BEST FRIEND 59
MARIA ROSA 62
ONE PATH AND MANY KEYS 64
THE TIMID SUN 66
MARINELLA 71

TERESINA THE SPIDER   75
THE COLOURED BALLOON   78
ANNA   80
GINO THE ELF   83
ROBERTO THE GLOBETROTTER   86
THE MAGIC CASKET   90
ELISA THE LITTLE ANT   92
THE ANGEL CALLED CHATTERBOX   94